W9-APV-107

Derek Desierto

Feiwel and Friends

New York

For anyone who has ever felt like an oddbird.

And for my nephews, Mateo and Lorenzo.

A FEIWEL AND FRIENDS BOOK
An imprint of Macmillan Publishing Group, LLC
120 Broadway, New York, NY 10271 • mackids.com

Library of Congress Control Number: 2020919761

First edition, 2021
Book design by Sharismar Rodriguez
Feiwel and Friends logo designed by Filomena Tuosto
Printed in China by RR Donnelley Asia Printing Solutions Ltd., Dongguan City, Guangdong Province

ISBN 978-1-250-86527-4 (special edition)
10 9 8 7 6 5 4 3 2 1

It was a hot day in the jungle.

The birds were at the pool.
But none of them were swimming.

All they cared about was showing off their fabulous feathers.

Then another bird appeared.
His feathers weren't colorful.
He was an oddbird.

And he was hot after a long flight to the pool.
He was excited to finally cool off.

As he dipped his toes into the water,
he felt everyone's eyes on him.

"He has no **color**," said one bird.
"Are those even *feathers*?" said another.

All the birds agreed that Oddbird didn't belong there.

Out!

Out!

Out!

Oddbird flew away as fast as he could.

He had always looked like this.
His feathers were his feathers.
Why was it a problem for
the other birds?

As he hopped around
the jungle, he noticed how
much color was all around him . . .

. . . and he had an idea!

Back at the pool, the birds were trying to relax when suddenly, there was a tweet in the crowd that someone new had arrived.

It was a *fabulous bird* with COLORS galore!

Oh my goodness, can you *believe* those feathers?
Look at that *blue.*
I *need* that fancy swimsuit.

Oddbird was so relieved! His new feathers meant that the other birds didn't recognize him. And they loved the way he looked!

Oddbird had never felt so confident.

He strutted to the diving board.
The other birds were shocked
and confused.

What about his gorgeous feathers?

From the top of the diving board, Oddbird counted . . .

One...

two...

three...

GO!

The water felt fine!
So cool! So refreshing!

Oddbird was so happy to swim that he didn't notice his "feathers" were falling off.

Is that...?

Oddbird was having too much fun to be worried.

Actually,
that looks
refreshing.

And *cool!*

One by one, the other birds jumped into the pool. Their feathers got frizzy. Their colors became dull.

But no one cared anymore about those things. What was more important was how they felt.

And they felt **happy.**

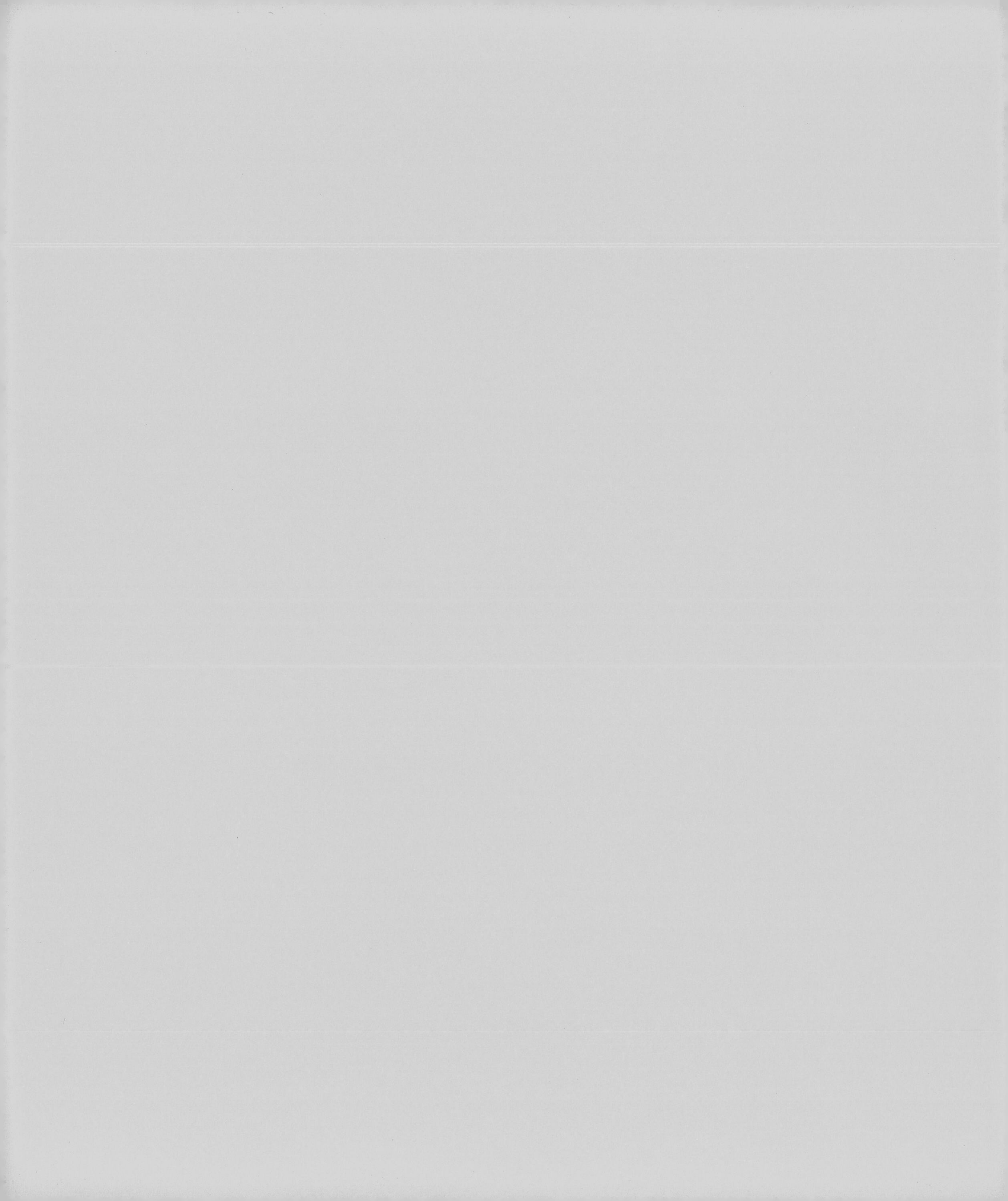